In The Eye Of The Family

Libelle Marcellus

Published by Libelle Marcellus, 2024.

IN THE EYE OF THE FAMILY

First edition. December 1, 2024.

Copyright © 2024 Libelle Marcellus.

ISBN: 979-8230425748

Written by Libelle Marcellus.

Table of Contents

Chapter One: This Is The Life; The Cool After The Storm

Momma was in the barn, carefully shaving some of the wool off the sheep we kept on the farm. The barn smelled of hay and the earthy scent of the animals, and the sound of the sheep's soft bleating filled the space as she worked. She moved with purpose, gathering the freshly cut wool into a woven basket at her feet. The cold bite of fall was in the air, and I could feel the crispness of winter creeping closer. Momma glanced over her shoulder at me and, with a sigh, said, "Lilac, gather some eggs from the chickens." She pointed to an empty basket with the tip of her boot.

I watched her for a moment, noticing how her hands moved with practiced ease, the way she worked without complaint despite the long hours. She was always doing something—whether it was tending to the animals, preparing food, or fixing things around the farm. The thought of winter made her more determined than ever, knowing we'd need warm clothes to last through the season. She had been talking about spinning the wool and making new clothes, and I could already feel the thick warmth of knitted wool in my mind, something I'd wear close to my skin to keep the cold away.

I wasn't sure if she gave me the task just to keep me busy so I wouldn't tug at her dress and trail after her all day, but I didn't mind. I liked the thought of being helpful, even if my chores were small compared to hers. "Alright, Momma," I said with a smile, grabbing the basket she pointed to, excited to do something on my own.

I made my way to the chicken coop, my boots crunching on the gravel path. The chickens clucked and flapped as I approached, their feathers ruffling in the chilly air. I opened the door and stepped inside, the familiar warmth of the coop wrapping around me like a blanket. The hens were busy pecking at the ground, their clucks of protest soft as I reached beneath them to collect the eggs. Some of the eggs were warm, and I could feel their soft curves in my hands as I placed them carefully in the basket. I loved this chore—it was simple but satisfying, like a small treasure hunt every time I gathered the eggs.

As I worked, I glanced back toward the barn. Momma was still busy, her back to me as she continued to prepare the wool. I felt proud to be helping her in my own way, even if it wasn't as important as the work she was doing. The sound of the chickens, the rustling of the wool in the barn, and the steady rhythm of my task filled the space around me, and for a moment, it felt like time was standing still. In the stillness of the afternoon, I found a sense of peace in the simple things—the warmth of the eggs in my basket, the soft clucking of the hens, and the promise of a warm winter ahead.

After I finished gathering the eggs, I went back to Momma.

That's when Momma gently told me to head back inside, where Poppa was waiting, and give him the basket of eggs so he could start cooking. I didn't hesitate, eager to help and play my part. The cool air of the morning brushed against my face as I made my way inside. Poppa was there, along with my older brother Jaimie. They had finished gathering plants from the grove and were now busy preparing them—sorting through the herbs for tea, medicine, and all the other recipes Poppa liked to make with the plants they found. The earthy smell of the herbs filled the room, mixing with the scent of the firewood crackling in the stove.

I approached Poppa with the basket of eggs, my tooth-gapped smile wide and proud. He gave me one of those knowing looks, the kind that said he didn't need to ask what I had brought him. Without a word, he took the basket and set it down, his hands already moving to start on the cheese omelet he was so good at making. The sizzle of the eggs in the pan was comforting, familiar. As the omelet took shape, I watched, feeling content with the small but meaningful task I had completed. My work for the day was done, so I made my way to the table, where Jaimie was busy sorting through the plants they had harvested. He carefully laid them out, organizing them by type—some for tea, others for medicine, and a few for recipes Momma would use for dinner.

I sat beside him, watching in silence as his hands moved with practiced precision. He didn't need to say much—he was always so focused on his work. I admired that about him. The room was filled with a quiet sense of purpose, the rhythmic sounds of chopping, stirring, and sorting blending into the peaceful hum of our little farm. I couldn't help but feel grateful for this simple life we lived.

As I sat there, watching the sunlight dance through the window, I thought to myself, *This is the life.* It wasn't glamorous or full of excitement, but it was real, it was ours, and it was exactly where I wanted to be. The work we did on the farm, the time we spent together, it all felt like something precious—something I didn't want to change.

Chapter Two: In The Eye Of The Family

I used to believe that I was terrified of change, but I was truly afraid of remaining in a place where I did not belong. Hurricane Irene was predicted to land in Port Capebot, Connecticut in just a few days. Following the last devastating hurricane that struck on Valentine's Day in 1970, this storm was forecasted to be the most severe to impact our city in the last 50 years.

When I first caught wind of the forecast regarding Hurricane Irene and the alarming predictions surrounding it, I couldn't help but scoff. It was clear to me that the exaggerated warnings about the storm's intensity stemmed from the reckless spending habits of the wealthy, who seem to care little for the environment.

Unfortunately, those with fewer resources always seem to bear the brunt of these disasters.

A few days before, the authorities had alerted our city, giving us ample time to leave. My family and I would leave Port Capebot to live with my Uncle Randy and my cousins in Saint Kapaal, North Carolina, which is a very long distance to drive outside the city.

We were a close-knit family of five, thriving on our farm. The farm had everything we needed.

The livestock, including cows, horses, pigs, and chickens, provided us with nourishing food to fill our stomachs and clothing to keep us warm. Just beyond the farm, a stunning grove flourished with vibrant plants, colorful flowers, and fresh vegetables. Poppa and I worked together, harmoniously guiding the livestock through various tasks on the farm. It was a complicated process that required meticulous attention to detail and a deep understanding of animal behavior. One of the key aspects we focused on was the importance of moving with care and patience, ensuring the animals felt comfortable and secure in our presence. Building trust was paramount, and being attuned to the slightest signs of fear or unease from the herd allowed us to adjust our approach accordingly. Establishing a connection with the animals meant respecting their flight zone, the boundary within which they felt most vulnerable and likely to flee. As Poppa imparted his knowledge and expertise, my elder brother Jaimie and I eagerly absorbed these lessons, eager to apply them in our exploration of plant life on the farm.

I was on a mission to gather plants for everyone. Momma, the expert on flora, was busy inside with our little brother Hayes. This left me with my older brother Jaimie, who was supposed to help me choose the right plants.

"That one...no, wait, that one," Jaimie kept insisting. It took every ounce of my patience to resist the urge to give him a good smack.

"Jaimie, why didn't you just grab the plant encyclopedia that Momma gave to you?" I exclaimed, my frustration evident.

"I'm not a fan of books," Jaimie replied nonchalantly.

"Even if you don't like them, we could have been back inside half an hour ago! You don't know anything about what you're doing!"

In my irritation, I reached for a handful of plants. Jaimie stared at me as if I had lost my mind. I picked up the plants to examine them in my hands, but after a few minutes, I then set them down, due to feeling an uncomfortable tingling sensation developing on my palm.

"Ouch!" I shouted, my voice echoing.

Mom rushed outside, alarmed by my cries, and hurried over to where Jaimie and I stood.

"What's happening out here?"

"We were trying to practice plant hunting," I explained. "But Jaimie wouldn't take the encyclopedia."

"I'm not interested in plant hunting. You two need to go back inside and start packing our things for evacuation."

Jaimie and I exchanged glances before turning back toward the house. As my older brother Jaimie and I stepped back into the house, I felt compelled to gaze at the family portrait adorning the wall. Mom and I, the only females in the family, were dressed in charming plaid dresses, while Dad, Jaimie, and our little brother were all clad in black.

Underneath the family photo, each of our names was carefully listed in order from oldest to youngest: Randolph, who we call Poppa; Kristen, who is Momma; Jaimie who is an elder brother; Lilac—that's me; and, last of all, baby boy Hayes.

The picture brought me back to times that were more peaceful in our family.

I took a moment to stare at that photo, and for a moment, I was in a different state of mind. It was a state of mind that gave me a sense of longing.

That moment of insight was abruptly shattered by the chaos unfolding behind me. Momma's voice rose in frustration as she yelled at us for lingering instead of actively helping to gather our things.

Poppa, my older brother, and I were under a lot of pressure from Momma to evacuate. She would continually check that we had our towels, hairbrushes, soaps, deodorants, toothpaste tubes, and whatnot. Momma's incessant worry was almost too much for me to cope with.

In times when I felt overwhelmed by stress, aside from immersing myself in my love for botany, I found solace in the enchanting world of poetry. Whenever this feeling of being excessively stressed crept up on me, I would retreat to the sanctuary of my room where my thoughts could flow freely.

During one of those quiet, reflective moments—the kind that sneak up on you when the sky turns that strange silver-gray before a storm—I thought about a girl from our neighborhood named Semi-Wolf. Her real name was Reece, but nobody called her that except her mom when she was mad. She got the name because her mother craved Reese's chocolates every day while she was pregnant. It made sense somehow—sweet but strong, just like her.

Semi-Wolf wanted to be a rapper and a poet. She wasn't famous or anything, but she carried herself like she already was. She had this way of talking that made everything sound like a verse, even if she was just asking someone to pass the hot sauce. I admired her, deeply. To me, she was the definition of cool—this fearless Black girl who didn't care what anyone thought. She had a kind of magnetic energy, like she knew who she was and didn't flinch when the world tried to tell her otherwise.

She was sixteen, four years older than me, and back then, that felt like a lifetime. I was only twelve—awkward and eager, still figuring out who I was—but I always wanted to impress her.

Not in a romantic way, just... I wanted her to see me. To take me seriously. To think I was cool too.

I remember making a decision right then. I slipped on my hoodie, pushed up my window, and climbed out into the cool air. The streetlights were buzzing faintly. The sky was heavy with clouds that looked like they were holding something back. My sneakers were almost silent against the sidewalk as I crept across the neighborhood, the hum of insects mixing with distant thunder.

When I got to her house, I hesitated for a second before knocking. My heart was thudding like a drum solo. Please let her be the one who answers, I thought.

And she was.

Semi-Wolf swung the door open, her presence just as loud as I remembered. She wore her signature look: black lipstick that popped against her dark skin, a gray beanie pulled low over her edges, baggy black pants that hung loose like she owned the wind, and a gray sports bra like she didn't care who stared. She looked like the future. Like rebellion and art and freedom rolled into one person.

"Randy!" she shouted, opening her arms wide.

"Semi-Wolf!" I shouted back, beaming.

We hugged, tight and warm and real. I hadn't seen her in a long time—not since the block party in June, when she freestyled over the DJ's beat and made the whole crowd cheer. Being in her presence again made the world feel sharper, more alive.

"You got a rhyme for me?" I asked, trying to sound casual, though I was bouncing inside.

She grinned. "Yeah! But this time, it's not a rap—it's a poem. A real one."

She didn't wait for me to say anything else.

She took a breath, closed her eyes for a second like she was tuning into a frequency no one else could hear, and then Semi-Wolf began:

January and February are the oldest of the few,

With the same fathers, but different mothers, they're the "uarys" through and through

They don't always see eye to eye but will agree when it's true

March, April, and May were born at different times, yet get along the most

With matching weather and temperatures, they have plenty to boast

June and July are twins, Geminis if you will

They're very antsy and youthful cherubs that can't keep still

August is the quiet one with has an introverted thrill

Then come the quadruplets with names ending in "ber"

September, October, November, and December, with matching last names, they have the same mother and father

"Wow, I like it, Van Gogh ."

"Thank you."

"Semi-Wolf, do you know about the oncoming hurricane?"

"Yeah, but me and my family aren't worried about it."

I gave Semi-Wolf a look, my brow scrunched. "Why aren't you worried about it? My whole family is trying to pack up and escape right now."

She shrugged, leaning against the doorway like it was no big deal. "Because we've been through storms before. Every year, there's one coming. They always say it's gonna be the big one, and half the time it changes direction or just fizzles out."

"But what if this one's different?" I asked, the nervousness rising in my voice.

Semi-Wolf looked at me for a long second, like she was deciding how much truth to give me.

"Maybe it is," she said. "But worry don't stop a storm. If it hits, it hits. We'll light some candles, play cards, and wait it out. That's how it is in this house."

There was something in the way she said it—like calm was a choice she had made a long time ago. Like she'd already seen things worse than a storm and decided they wouldn't break her.

I glanced past her shoulder into the house. I could hear the sound of pots clanking, the faint beat of a hip-hop instrumental playing from a speaker, and someone laughing in another room.

My house, in contrast, felt like it was breaking apart—boxes everywhere, the TV blaring storm coverage, my mom snapping at my dad, and Newborn crying in the corner.

I looked back at Semi-Wolf.

"I just hope y'all don't die or get flattened like pancakes. That would ruin my week."

The words hung in the air heavier than I meant them to. Semi-Wolf's smile faded just a little—not gone, but dimmed, like someone had turned the volume down on her energy.

She didn't flinch. She just looked at me.

"Damn, Randy," she said, crossing her arms loosely. "You always say what's on your mind, huh?"

"I'm serious," I replied. "I don't want to find out later that your house got swept away or your roof collapsed or—or something worse. I don't want you to be a person I only remember."

For a second, she didn't say anything. Just studied me.

Then she stepped out onto the porch, closer to where I was standing.

"We're not dying," she said firmly, but not angrily. "That's not how our story ends."

A breeze pushed past us, fast and cool, brushing her braids against her face. The clouds above were darker now, swirling like smoke in a pot that had been left too long on the stove.

She looked up at the sky for a moment, then back at me.

"You really care, huh?"

"Yeah," I said. "I do."

She nodded slowly, then bumped her shoulder into mine.

"That's sweet of you, Randy. But don't worry. Semi-Wolf doesn't go down easy."

And even though the wind picked up and thunder cracked somewhere in the distance, something about her voice made me believe it.

I made my way back home, slipping through the shadows like I was on a secret mission. I climbed back into my room through the same window I had snuck out of. My feet hit the floor without a sound.

No one saw me. Good.

I barely had time to exhale, thinking I'd pulled it off clean—when the door flew open like it had been kicked by the wind.

Momma burst into the room, eyes blazing, and started scolding me like she'd been saving it up all night.

Then, with a more friendly demeanor, she reminded me that it was time to tidy up for the day and prepare for the upcoming journey. Momma was bipolar like that.

I started thinking about Semi-Wolf again. I deeply wished that my words could offer solace to someone, similar to the comforting effect her words had on me. However, battling an overwhelming sense of stage fright, I found myself grappling with insecurity. This feeling of unease seemed to stem from the negative narrative my mother often spoke of, painting a picture of a world filled with people harboring ill intentions toward my brother and me. As I mulled over these sentiments, an underlying fear began to gnaw at me, reinforcing the cautions issued by my mother and planting seeds of doubt in my mind about the trustworthiness of those around us. The weight of these fearful notions lingered like a heavy cloud overhead, casting a shadow on my ability to step into the limelight and share my own words of solace.

When I was younger, Mom would never allow me to visit other people's homes for fear of something awful happening to me. She is very protective of my older brother and me, but I believe this balances out because Poppa is a much more laid-back parent.

He was certainly less concerned about how he would influence my older brother and me. He frequently smoked in the house when I was a child. Because of that, Momma and Poppa used to argue frequently. Poppa now only smokes outside the house, but I can still see him from my bedroom window when he does it. I did think Momma's criticism of Poppa's smoking habits was a little hypocritical since she used to take cocaine. She even experienced a miscarriage as a result of it, but I was never going to confront her about it.

I always wondered if Momma's overprotectiveness came from guilt. Because of Poppa, my older brother started smoking when he was just eleven years old. When Momma learned about his smoking habit, Jaimie vowed to never smoke again and insisted that it was not an addiction. I'm not sure how much of that was genuine because I saw him smuggle a Mr. Miskey box into his luggage as we were packing ready to depart Port Capebot. Mr. Miskey's boxes were vintage-styled and depicted the rough hands of a man lighting a cigarette on the boxes.

I guess the company that produces these cigarettes did this to avoid any potential lawsuits about misleading consumers. There was a strong possibility that we would end up living with Uncle Randy and my other cousins for a while long after the hurricane made landfall. I personally really didn't care whether we were hit by any storm. Even though I didn't particularly enjoy living in Port Capebot. There were potholes everywhere on the street because the government didn't care enough to invest money into the city. Still, I knew no other cities but that one. Before this, neither my family nor I had ever ventured beyond the city. We lacked the resources since we were impoverished. I had the impression that I had lived the majority of my life inside a bubble.

And I wasn't going to be the one to pop it myself. Everyone got into the car, and I had to sit on the far left since the middle seat was intended for my younger brother, Newborn. He was about three months old, and we still hadn't come up with a name for him. I had seen his birth certificate before, and near his name, it said "baby boy Hayes" because that was my mother's last name. Momma and Poppa were never married, claimed to be connected "spiritually," and said that marriage is merely a piece of paper.

Hayes was a cute baby who hardly ever screamed and was rather calm for his age. He looked like a cherub because of his extra chubby and brown cheeks. Momma wanted us to leave the area early to avoid the unpleasant inconvenience of traffic. The distance required to get there was considerable. This was probably the first time I had ever taken a road trip. I honestly did not know what to expect.

When we were on the road, the highway seemed endless, as if it would go on forever. It made me glad that I took my Auto Race game with me to kill time. Or else I probably would have just screamed at everybody else in this car.

"How much longer till we get to Randy's?" Jaimie yelled.

"We will get there when we get there!" Poppa screamed back.

"Why do I smell cigarettes in this car?" Momma asked and she turned her head to Poppa, assuming the cigarette smell was coming from him. When she found it was not the case she turned her head to Jaimie. It was almost like he could feel Momma's inner thoughts because he looked scared. It was almost as if he knew what Momma was thinking about doing to him.

All of a sudden, Papa threatened to take away Jaimie's cigarette packets in the car - and then they got into a screaming match. Newborn was sleeping peacefully in the backseat but then Jamie and Poppa's screaming match made him wake up and erupt into a crying fit. I didn't blame him. I wish that sometimes I was a newborn too, so my feelings could be understood. But

I'm much older, so I doubt people would be as understanding if I started crying like that.

I tilted my head back against the seat and sighed. This was going to be a very long trip.

Chapter Three: Ashy Knees

We continued our journey in the car, the road stretching endlessly ahead of us. The trip from Porte Capebot, located in Connecticut to Saint Kapaal, North Carolina was going to take at least 12 hours, and we knew we'd need to make several stops along the way, which would only extend our travel time to Uncle Randy's.

I was comfortably settled in my seat next to baby boy Hayes when I felt that familiar, irritating scratch on the palm of my hand. This time, though, the itch was worse than before—sharper, almost burning. I glanced down and noticed a pink and red spotted rash spreading across my skin, and a gasp escaped from my mouth before I could stop it.

"What's wrong?" Poppa asked, catching my expression in the rearview mirror.

"Nothing," I replied quickly, hiding my hands in my lap.

But Jaimie, always sticking his nose where it doesn't belong, leaned over and squinted at my hand. "She's got poison ivy on her hands!" he yelled, loud enough to turn heads.

Momma spun around, eyes narrowing. "Lilac, what did you do to your hands?"

I stayed silent for a moment, not sure how to respond. Then Momma kept hammering me with the question again.

"don't know," I muttered, the guilt settling in my chest. I hated that I was becoming sick—it made me feel like a liability.

Finally, I remembered earlier, when Jaimie and I were trying to pick out plants. I'd brushed against something, and the sting had shot through the palm of my hands, leaving me with poison ivy. It made me shoot a dirty look at elder brother Jaimie.

"What are you looking at me like that for?" Jaimie asked in a stupid tone of voice.

I simply sighed and looked away from him. I wasn't in the mood to be starting an argument with him, or anyone else for that matter. Resigned to the tension lingering in the air, I absentmindedly went back to scratching the palm of my hands, the rasp of my nails against my skin a subtle backdrop to the heavy silence. Poppa, perceptive as ever, must have heard the faint sound of my nails grazing my palm over the sound of the car engine. His concerned voice cut through the quiet, "We're gonna need to go to a hospital for that," he said, his worry palpable in the way his hands gripped the steering wheel.

I leaned back in my seat, the creak of the old chair a familiar comfort as Poppa's words sunk in. His mention of hospitals triggered a pang of guilt within me, a weight that stemmed from the strain it often caused between our parents when Jaimie and I fell ill. It wasn't just the tension in their relationship that preyed on my mind, but also my deep-seated fear of needles. I can vividly recall my childhood antics of seeking refuge under waiting room chairs to escape the dreaded prick of a vaccine injection. Those days seem distant now, relegated to a time when innocence shielded me from the harsh realities of medical visits. But as time advanced and maturity settled in, I knew that confronting my fears was inevitable. The prospect of setting foot in a hospital still sent shivers down my spine, yet the resolve to seek help when needed overshadowed those trepidations. Age had brought a degree of wisdom that urged me to face adversity head-on, even if it meant embracing the discomfort that lurked within the sterile walls of healthcare facilities.

After a moment of more driving, Poppa had to hit the brakes hard, having spotted something in the road. Jaimie and I lurched forward in our seats as the car came to a sudden halt.

"What was that all about?!" Jaimie exclaimed, clearly annoyed.

"I saw a child in the road," Poppa replied, trying to explain himself.

I had to perk up out of my seat to have a better look, and indeed. There was a child sprawled out in the center of the road, but as soon as he noticed our car had halted for him, he sprang to his feet and walked away. A heavy silence enveloped the car for a few moments.

"Should we go after him to check if he's okay?" Momma inquired.

"Not! That kid must be out of his mind. Who just lies down in the road without a reason?" Jaimie retorted.

"Jaimie, be quiet," Momma snapped back, still irritated with him for smoking earlier.

Poppa let out a resigned sigh and steered the car to the roadside.

"I'm going to see where he went," Poppa declared.

What do you want us to do? Momma inquired of Poppa.

"You can join me if you'd like," Poppa responded. "I shouldn't be too long."

We all unfastened our seatbelts, exited the car, and began to follow him as a family, eager to see where the child might have gone. It wasn't long before we arrived at a quaint single-story house surrounded by a lush garden filled with various herbs.

I approached the door, but as I knocked, I noticed Poppa suddenly seemed eager to return to the car.

"What's bothering you?" Momma questioned him.

"I think we should go back," Poppa insisted.

"Why's that?" Momma pressed.

"I recognize this garden..." Poppa's voice trailed off, leaving an air of mystery.

I glanced back at Momma and Poppa, who seemed as though they were deep in discussion. With a shrug, I knocked on the door again, determined to see what lay beyond.

The woman who opened the door was adorned with a headscarf, a nose ring, and intricate black tattoos that covered her skin.

As soon as she appeared, Poppa inhaled sharply.

"Hello," she greeted, her tone direct. "What do you need?"

"We noticed a child lying in the middle of the road and wanted to check if he was okay," Momma explained, cradling Hayes in her arms.

The woman let out a sigh, her irritation evident.

"Yes, that's Junior. He's fine."

"So, you just allow your kids to play in the street?" Momma asked the woman.

The woman paused, carefully observing Momma with keen interest before she finally responded. "I apologize for any inconvenience, but this particular area tends to be rather secluded, resulting in a lot of minimal traffic," she disclosed, her tone carrying a subtle hint of superiority. Sensing a subtle change in the atmosphere, Poppa gently grasped Momma's arm, suggesting they make their exit. Catching this exchange, Momma glanced briefly at Poppa, only to be surprised when the woman directed a warm, welcoming smile toward him. "Hey there, Randolph! What a beautiful family you have," she exclaimed cheerfully. Shocked, Momma turned to Poppa with wide eyes, her initial confusion giving way to a mix of surprise and disbelief. "Randolph?!" she gasped in astonishment, seeking clarification from Poppa. "You know this woman?!" Taken aback by the unexpected turn of events, Poppa let out a resigned sigh before revealing the truth. "Yes, her name is Ashneed. She was someone I used to date in the past," he admitted, the weight of his confession hanging heavy in the air. Meanwhile, me and Jaimie simply stared at the three of them in silence, unsure of whether or not we were allowed to butt in "grown folks business." It seemed as though Poppa and Ashneed had a history with each other.

While my elder brother and Jaimie exchanged glances at each other, I felt that same pang on the palm of my hand again. I look down at the rash on my hand and begin to scratch it. The woman notices my actions and her expression shifts to one of concern.

"What happened to the baby's hand?" she asks, her voice laced with worry.

"She got the rash from playing with poison ivy," Jaimie replies.

I shot Jaimie an annoyed expression on my face, annoyed that he was making it sound like I carelessly touched the poisonous plants when it was really his fault I ended up with this rash.

"We were on our way to the hospital anyway," Poppa adds.

"No, it's fine, I can prepare something for her hand right now," the woman insists.

We exchange glances, and then, as a group, we follow her inside. She leads us to a table where we can sit.

"Junior!" the woman calls out in a sharp tone, and soon after, the boy we saw lying down on the street earlier appears "Retrieve the plants from the garden, please. "

She directed, and the child promptly obeyed, heading off to fulfill her request.

"It will only take me a moment to prepare for this. Would you care for some sandwiches?"

The woman inquired warmly.

"No, thank you—" the mother attempted to respond, but Jaimie quickly interjected.

"Yes, please! I would love some sandwiches."

Momma shot a disapproving glance at Jaimie, yet the woman simply smiled at him.

"Absolutely." With that, she rose and began preparing sandwiches for everyone. She placed the sandwiches on plates in front of us at the table, just as Junior returned.

"Thank you! That took you long enough," the woman remarked to the child.

The child was then shooed away to go watch TV in the living room. The house was covered with ancestral artifacts.

The woman retrieved a mortar and pestle and began to grind the herbs together. As a family, we gathered around, observing her work. Jaimie was the first to dig into the sandwiches. The woman mixed the herbs, and the pungent smell filled the room, a blend of earthy scents that reminded me of the farm.

It was a stark contrast to the anxiety lingering from our evacuation preparations and the uncertainty of Hurricane Irene looming over our heads.

"Is this your first time in Raven's Reach?" she asked, glancing at us over her shoulder.

I nodded, unsure of how to articulate the jumble of emotions swirling within me.

"It's a quiet place," she continued. "Sometimes too quiet, but it has its charm. You'll see."

Poppa shifted in his seat, casting a nervous glance at Momma. I could tell he was itching to leave, but curiosity held him back, just as it held me.

"What do you grow in your garden?" I asked, hoping to steer the conversation away from any uncomfortable history between my father and this woman.

"Oh, a little bit of everything," she replied with a smile. "Herbs, vegetables, flowers. My son and I like to experiment. It keeps us busy, especially when storms are brewing."

"Do you ever get storms out here?" Jaimie chimed in, taking a bite of his sandwich.

"Not like you're facing now," she said, shaking her head. "But I've learned to be prepared. Always have a plan, and always have supplies ready. You never know what nature has in store."

Her words sent a shiver down my spine, reminding me of the urgency in Momma's tone as she rushed to pack everything we might need.

"I hope we don't have to stay long," I whispered, half to myself.

Momma turned to me, her brow furrowed. "What do you mean, sweet pea?"

"I just... I don't know how long we'll be here. What if we can't go back home? I don't want to leave the farm forever."

Momma's expression softened, and she reached across the table to squeeze my hand. "We'll figure it out, honey. We're a family, and families stick together."

I wanted to believe her, but uncertainty clung to my thoughts.

Just then, Junior returned from the living room, his eyes wide with curiosity. "What are you all talking about?"

"Just about the storm and how we're all going to stay safe," Momma replied.

He nodded solemnly, then turned to his mother. "Can I help with the plants?"

"Of course, but be careful not to touch the poison ivy!" she warned, her voice lightening the moment.

After some time, the woman completed her mixture and applied it to my hands.

"Wow! Thank you!" I exclaimed.

"You're welcome, dear," the woman replied.

The irritating itchy sensation that had been bothering me on the palm of my hand suddenly vanished into thin air, leaving me feeling as though it had never been there in the first place. The relief I felt was akin to experiencing a touch of magic as if some invisible force had come to my aid and granted me instant comfort. I could already feel this moment becoming stitched into my memory like fabric.

"I could have managed that on my own," Momma remarked, displaying a hint of envy towards Ashneed.

"Yeah, but you didn't," Jaimie said to Momma. Momma simply stared at him for a moment and rolled her eyes at him. It struck me as somewhat ironic that my mother appeared to harbor a dislike for the woman, especially considering the numerous similarities they shared. My father seemed to have a preference for women who were knowledgeable in botany. I am convinced that had it not been for their prior relationship with Randolph, they might have formed a close friendship.

Poppa shifted around in his chair uncomfortably, casting sideways glances at the woman, Ashneed, whose calm, knowing smile hinted at unspoken memories shared between the two of them.

"You know, there are some things that you can't leave behind, Randolph," Ashneed said with a snide smile to Poppa.

Momma turned to the woman and said,

"I must admit, I'm still grateful you chose to help my child." Her tone carried a slight edge.

"Certainly, I bear no grudges."

"Oh? You don't?"

"No, because if I did, my spells wouldn't be as effective. The ancestors don't like it when you hold grudges."

Momma looked at the woman with eyes full of shock. "Spells? Are you a witch?" Asheneed simply laughed at Momma's comment.

"No, but I honestly wish I was. I'm a herbalist."

"Oh? I'm a herbalist too."

"Yes, I figured. Keep on working at it."

We all got back inside the car.

There was once again a moment of silence between all of us. I was still looking down at the palm of my hand, amazed at how quickly the rash on my hand seemed to have gone away. Momma never came up with a herbal recipe as strong as that. Still, I understood the importance of keeping that opinion to myself, particularly at this moment when tensions were palpable among us all.

"You never mentioned that you had an ex-girlfriend," Momma remarked to Poppa while we were in the car.

Jaimie and I exchanged glances and sighed, silently communicating our shared sentiment of "Here we go again." It seemed that just when a semblance of tranquility emerged within the family, someone inevitably felt compelled to disrupt the peace once more.

Poppa replied, "I did not believe it was necessary." He avoided making eye contact with Momma. I did not blame Poppa for the way he responded to Momma. There was no purpose to disclose one's entire life narrative, including all previous relationships, to a partner. This seems particularly irrelevant when encountering those individuals again is not expected.

Momma chuckled. "And what's that woman's name again? Ashneed?"

"Yes"

"Her name sounds hideous. Did her parents name her that because she has ashy knees?"

"No, I think her parents named her that because they thought it was a beautiful name and they loved their daughter."

Momma simply huffed and sat back in her chair.

I was not mad at him for vaguely defending Ashneed. I was so thankful for Momma deciding to drop the whole conversation right there. Poppa and the woman weren't even flirting with each other. He seemed as though, in fact, he appeared eager to wrap up the interaction swiftly. With a hurricane that was as serious as Irene threatening on the horizon, the last thing we needed was for Momma and Poppa to be arguing in the car about a relationship that was long gone.

Chapter Four: Kristen, The Model

The journey in the car continued for several more hours under the changing hues of the sky as the sun slowly descended beyond the horizon. We made a necessary stop at the gas stations along the way. The scent of gasoline and freshly brewed coffee wafted through the air, a comforting familiarity amid the vast unknown of the open road.

As the car journey continued, there was an unassuming quality, with the scenery outside zipping by calmly. It was a typical drive until it came to a halt unexpectedly in front of a gas station adjacent to a dress store. The captivating display in the window caught Momma's attention, a poster featuring a woman exuding elegance in an off-the-shoulder blue dress adorned with delicate ruffles at the hem. The woman's radiant smile and confident pose resonated with a familiar charm resembling Momma's essence.

She wore her natural hair out, a full, voluminous Afro that framed her face with a beautiful, curly texture, each coil standing out in its unique pattern. The rich, textured curls added a striking contrast to her features, exuding both confidence and effortless style.

A moment of realization sparked when Momma, with an amused expression, pointed to the poster and exclaimed gleefully, "Hey look, that's me!" It was a delightful surprise to discover that the woman depicted in the poster was indeed Momma herself, capturing her beauty and spirit in such a striking manner that even she couldn't help but be amazed by the resemblance. Momma decided to walk inside the dressing store.

Poppa was outside the car pumping gas, but my elder brother Jaimie decided to follow Momma inside the dress store.

Momma, with slight apprehension, approached a woman in the store, her eyes narrowing with curiosity as she studied the features that seemed so familiar. "Hey," she ventured, voice tinged with uncertainty, "that woman on the poster is me." The words hung in the air, waiting for acknowledgment, but the woman had yet to turn around, her focus seemingly elsewhere. Momma's eyes darted around the store, taking in the cozy aroma of freshly brewed coffee and the soft hum of background chatter as she waited for a response.

Finally, the woman behind the counter turned to face Momma, her eyes lighting up with a mixture of recognition and warmth. "Yes, I know," she replied softly, a small smile playing on her lips. Momma's heart skipped a beat as she caught sight of a photo tucked away on the counter - a snapshot frozen in time of a younger version of herself wrapped in a loving embrace. The pieces began to click into place, understanding dawning on her as she realized the depth of the connection between them.

At that moment, the woman's face lit up with joy as she turned fully towards Momma, her eyes sparkling with emotion. "My beautiful Kristen!" she exclaimed, the words filled with a sense of nostalgia and familiarity that tugged at Momma's heartstrings. Kristen felt a rush of emotions flooding over her, a sense of belonging and recognition washing over her as she embraced the woman before her, the shared history and unspoken bond weaving between them like an invisible thread that had connected their lives in unexpected ways.

"My beautiful little model!" The woman at the counter remarked, her voice full of pride.

"Model?" I asked, unable to keep the question from slipping out.

Momma turned toward me, her lips curling into a gentle smile. "Yes, honey. I used to be a runaway model."

"Your mother had one of the most promising careers in modeling," the woman at the counter added, nodding as she spoke. "I've known her since she was a baby. I was the one who scouted her for an agency."

"Oh, so you know who momma is?" Jaimie asked, raising an eyebrow.

The woman's eyes softened as she nodded her head. "I was the one who adopted her from a small island and brought her to the U.S."

After the woman behind the counter explained the backstory of how she knew our mom, I noticed another photo tucked behind the register. It was a picture of her, Momma, and a bunch of guys who looked like they belonged in a rock band. The men had their faces painted white, with dark makeup ringing around their eyes. They all held guitars, and one of them even had his arm draped around Momma. Among the musicians stood Travis Velvet, who I instantly recognized. The band comprised members named Love Velvet, Trash Velvet, Sky Velvet, and Little Velvet - it was a lineup where each artist adopted the Velvet surname. It wasn't because they were related though. It was because they wanted to show their unity as a group. Travis Velvet was the third guitar player in the group and he had a very slender build, he was associated with the color blue during their performances.

"Hey, that looks like *The Velvet Missiles*!" I exclaimed, unable to hide my excitement. The woman glanced back at the photo I was pointing to, a small smile on her face.

"Yes, that is *The Velvet Missiles,*" she confirmed with a nod.

Momma laughed, her expression a mix of amusement and nostalgia. "Yes, honey, that was my boyfriend before I met your father."

I stared at her in disbelief. "*The Velvet Missiles* were my favorite band of all time! I've done so much research on them."

I paused, my eyes lingering on the photo once again, as if trying to absorb every detail. It was hard to fully grasp what I was seeing—everything felt like it needed a moment to sink in.

"So you used to date one of the members? Before you met Poppa?" I asked, my voice barely above a whisper, still trying to take in this unexpected piece of family history.

The Velvet Missiles weren't just any band. They were one of the most iconic rock groups of the '70s. Their name was inspired by the political turmoil of the previous decade — the Cold War, missile crises, and the threat of looming disaster. Protests and counter-culture movements had swept the world as people cried out for peace. The band's lead singer, captivated by this clash of power and gentleness, came up with *The Velvet Missiles* after watching a protest where demonstrators waved velvet-colored flowers while chanting against the "missiles in the sky." The "velvet" symbolized the soft resistance of peace movements, and "missiles" reflected the force of government power. They wanted their music to embody that same tension: powerful, like a missile, yet as smooth and subversive as velvet.

"Wow," I murmured, still stunned. Seeing Momma, always so grounded and practical, connected to such an intense, rebellious part of history was truly a revelation.

Jaimie jumped in with his usual curiosity. "So, what happened, Momma? Why didn't you keep modeling?"

The woman's gaze shifted, her voice suddenly much quieter. "She met your father," she said bluntly, her words carrying a weight that hung in the air.

Momma laughed softly, but I could see the bittersweetness behind her smile. There was a heaviness in her eyes—an unspoken history I hadn't fully understood until that moment. It was a story with women that was all too common.

They would have promising careers and ambitions all for them to be ruined by a man and children. It was especially hurtful when the man the woman halted her career to have children with didn't have a lot of things going for himself. I looked out the window of the shop, seeing Poppa, still pumping gas in the car.

Poppa wasn't a bad man, not by any means, but he wasn't remarkable either. He lived simply and honestly, never seeking to take from others. As a farmer, he made a steady living, working the land he'd inherited from his family, tending to it with the same quiet diligence that had been passed down through generations.

Still, the Velvet Missiles were my favorite music band of all time, so it was insane for me to think that one of the members could have been my father, making the other members my uncles. It made me start to wonder what momma saw in Poppa, which was so good that she was willing to forgo her path to becoming a model and the wife of a musician just to be with him.

It was a question that started to burn into my mind as I processed all of this information.

I didn't mind it at all — if momma met Poppa and decided to date him more. It was more so that Poppa was boring and was nothing extraordinary. I let out a deep sigh. After Momma and the woman reconnected and talked more about their memories, we all got back inside the car.

Silence fell over us once again, thick and heavy like the storm clouds gathering outside. Poppa reached for the radio, his hands tense as he turned the dial. A static crackle filled the room before the broadcaster's voice cut through, sharp and urgent.

"Hurricane Irene," the announcer said, his tone grave. "Projected to intensify, with winds up to 115 miles per hour, battering everything in its path." I could feel a shiver go down my spine as he detailed the hurricane's relentless approach, its strength, its hunger.

Outside, the wind began to howl, rattling the windows as if eager to break through. I glanced around, catching the fear in everyone's eyes. Irene was coming closer, fierce and unforgiving, a force of nature that we were powerless to stop. It was no longer just news; it was a presence, bearing down on us, filling every corner of the room with a quiet, luminous danger that felt impossible to escape.

Poppa turned up the volume as the anchor continued, his voice almost drowned out by the sound of rain pelting against the roof, each drop tapping out an anxious rhythm. "With every passing hour, Irene's trajectory is narrowing. We're now looking at a likely landfall by tonight. We cannot stress enough—prepare for power outages, severe flooding, and debris. This storm has the potential to devastate everything in its path."

I looked at Poppa, who stared at the radio with an expression I'd never seen before. His usual calm resolve was cracked, and the fear in his eyes mirrored what I felt building in my chest. The reality was sinking in: Irene was no longer a distant threat. It was coming, relentless and indifferent, its fury bound to sweep over everything we knew, leaving who knew what in its wake.

Chapter Five: The Sunset Lodge Inn

We were on the road, listening to a song called "Cosmic Identity Crisis" by The Velvet Missiles. The lyrics went something like this:

Which planet am I?
When I find myself grounded by the soil
I look up at this vast cosmic tapestry and wonder where I lie
And question if planets have their inner turmoil
Would I be Pluto,
The one appears so insignificant,
They become isolated from the clan
When it comes down to it, we are not so different
But I am pushed away, so alone is where I stand
Possibly I am Neptune,
The one that is so mysterious,
With vast and great lands yet to be explored
So surreal and so oblivious
But as an outer layer so recognized and can be adored
An aura waiting to be discovered,
There is so much more than what is covered
Which planet am I?
I could be Uranus,
The one tilted on its side
I find it hard to keep my balance
Or color inside of the lines
But I can handle it when it happens
Should I be Saturn,
The one with plenty of rings,

Looking for love wherever I go,
I can feel my heart opening,
For that person who will love me so
I too, wear devotion on my sleeve
But I can still pick up the rest of me
Which planet am I?
I am probably Jupiter,
The one who is the largest,
That is the size of my pride sometimes,
When it could be more modest,
On occasion, it can be hard to read between the lines
Maybe I am Mars,
The one with so much potential,
But just needs extra effort
To be truly influential
I know that I can be something better
Which planet am I?
Perhaps I am the Earth
The one brimming with life,
In the right zone, I come alive,
But if not, then it is truly a strife
The right standing gives me the qualities for which I am
renown
Surely I must be Venus,
The one too similar to "her",
But at the same time is too distinct
So lines start to become a blur
When our orbits start to interlink
She is more full of life than I
Others say I'm too harsh and should try to be habitable,

It hurts because I already try
Which planet am I?
I might also be Mercury
The one closest to the sun,
I thrive in the warmer climates
I soak the heat as a sponge,
Only those built for it can survive it
So, which planet am I?
Each one of the planets has a special place in my heart
They are all traits in which I can confide
And it has been like that since the start
Instead of being defined by only some
I am an amalgamation of all of them
My essence in the stars ebbs and flows between
And make up something way bigger than the world painted
the picture to be

The soft, mellow tones filled the car, creating a sense of calm that felt strangely out of place. Outside, the world was anything but serene—dark clouds loomed overhead, and rain hammered against the windshield in relentless sheets. The wind whipped trees into a frantic dance, their branches clawing at the air as if they, too, were trying to escape the chaos.

Inside the car, though, it was as if time had slowed. The soothing melody wrapped around us, cocooning us in a fragile bubble of peace. I glanced over at the others. Mom was gripping the steering wheel a little tighter than usual, her eyes fixed on the road ahead, while Dad tapped his fingers absentmindedly on his leg, keeping time with the rhythm. Even Lilac, usually a bundle of energy, sat quietly, staring out at the storm with an expression I couldn't quite place—part wonder, part worry.

It felt surreal, like we were caught between two worlds: the storm raging outside and the serenity of that song. For a moment, I wondered which one would win.

The storm outside the car was starting to pick up as the rain beat down relentlessly on the windshield. The wind let out a whistling howl so loud it drowned out any other sound. Despite the intensifying weather conditions, we all sat in silence, each lost in our thoughts, the tension growing palpable inside the car. It was as if the storm mirrored the turmoil within us, the uncertainty and fear blending seamlessly with the chaos outside.

The road stretched out endlessly before us, disappearing into the darkness that was only punctuated by occasional flashes of lightning that illuminated the landscape in eerie, brief moments of clarity. Still, the car pressed forward, the engine's steady hum which was sort of reassuring against the chaos of Hurricane Irene.

Then, without warning, a deafening crash shattered the eerie calm that had settled in the car. Metal scraped against metal, an unsettling sound that seemed to echo through the vehicle. Poppa's hands tightened on the steering wheel, a tense silence enveloping us as we all shared a moment of collective alarm. It was at that moment that he finally decided to pull over. Luckily, in the distance, we saw a sign of a Holiday Inn ahead offering a beacon of hope in the swirling darkness with its name flickering in neon lights: **Sunset Lodge Inn**.

Poppa rolled the car to a stop in the hotel parking lot, and a sense of relief washed over us, mingling with the lingering tension that still hung heavy in the air. We filed out of the car, each of us weary and damp from the relentless storm, grateful for the promise of shelter and respite from the turbulent night.

Poppa's weary gaze met mine, a silent acknowledgment passing between us that sometimes, bravery meant knowing when to seek sanctuary in the face of adversity.

We checked into the hotel, and the warmth of the lobby felt as though it was enveloping us in its embrace after the harshness of the storm.

A woman stood behind the reception desk as Poppa approached her.

"Is there any chance we could get a room for the night?" he asked, sounding hopeful. "I know reservations usually need to be made in advance, but there's a storm outside—Hurricane Irene is coming through, and—"

The woman gave a polite smile and cut in, "Yes, we can accommodate you."

Poppa sighed with relief. "I'm assuming you'd like a two-bedroom suite?" she asked.

He nodded.

"Alright, let me check with my supervisor to confirm availability." She slipped through a door. We were left amongst ourselves for a while, waiting for a response.

Curious and in need of a distraction, I made the spontaneous decision to shift my attention toward the poster displayed on the plain, unadorned wall of the room. While I typically shied away from reading unless it was an assignment given by my school, at that moment, my usual aversion held no weight over me. Peering intently at the poster's depiction, an image of a man with a fair complexion, swaths of blonde hair cascading stylishly, clothed in a sophisticated tan suit, caught my eye. In a stance that exuded confidence and pride, he stood with arms crossed, emanating an aura of authority. The man was known as Hank Waverly, the owner of the Sunset Lodge Inn. The man appeared amiable and down-to-earth, possessing a rugged charm that hinted at his roots in a quaint, small town. Observing his posture and expression, it was not difficult to envision him as a hands-on figure actively involved in the day-to-day management of the hotel, embodying the quintessential persona of a welcoming and engaging host.

The woman returned shortly after, handing us the room keys. "Room 305 on the third floor," she said, smiling.

We took the elevator up, grateful to have found shelter for the night. Once we got to our room, we dropped our bags and took a moment to relax.

"I'm so glad she was kind enough to let us stay," Momma said, visibly relieved.

Jaimie's stomach growled loudly. "I'm hungry," she announced.

"Good thing there's a buffet downstairs," Poppa replied with a grin.

Jaimie was right; I was pretty hungry too. With everything that had been going on in the family, I'd almost forgotten my last proper meal. We headed downstairs, to the cafeteria, which hosted the extravagant buffet. The room exuded a sense of opulence and vastness. Massive, ornate golden chandeliers adorned the high ceilings, casting a warm, inviting glow over the elegant setting. The wooden tables, complemented by chairs adorned with plush green and red cushions, added a touch of sophistication and comfort to the entire dining experience. The overall ambiance created a luxurious and inviting atmosphere that made dining a truly memorable and enjoyable experience for all patrons.

We found a grand buffet spread full of choices—macaroni, vegetables, meats, and more. The sight of it made our stomachs rumble in unison, and we eagerly filled our plates, grateful for the warm meal after such a long day.

We were standing in line to pay for our food—or rather, Papa was, mostly. But just then, he remembered he'd left his debit card in Momma's wallet. Papa asked her for it, knowing that's where he'd put the card. As he searched through her wallet, a photo slipped out. It was a picture of her and Travis Velvet, hugging.

Papa didn't say anything right then. He waited until we were all seated. Then, he asked Momma to step aside with him near the bathrooms for a private conversation. My older brother, Jaimie, and I decided to be nosy and watched them from a distance. Jaimie was holding baby Hayes.

"Kristen, be honest with me—do you have a photo of Travis Velvet in your wallet?" Papa asked quietly.

Momma looked at him with an expression of surprise and irritation, as if he'd crossed a line just by asking.

"Is that any of your business?" she replied with a sharp tone.

"I just need to know."

"And what if I do?" she snapped. "It's not like I have a chance with him anymore anyway."

"Maybe not," Papa said, "but keeping that photo means you're still thinking about him."

"Does it bother you that I think about him?"

"Yes! It does!"

"May I please ask why?"

"You insulted my ex-girlfriend Ashneed by saying her name was similar to "ashy knees. You said that it bothered you for some reason that I used to be with her, so why am I not allowed to be bothered if you still think about Travis Velvet?"

"That's not the same thing."

"Oh really? Please tell me why it's not the same thing."

They stood there, locked in a tense silence. Finally, Momma's expression hardened.

"I'm so disgusted with you right now," she said, ending the conversation. She turned and walked back to our table at the buffet without another word. When Momma walks away like that, you know the conversation is over.

"Damn," Jaimie said, looking over at me.

Momma's steps were heavy as she made her way back to our table at the buffet, clearly indicating her deep disappointment and frustration. Her silence was deafening, the unspoken tension lingering in the air like a thick fog. It was as if every unspoken word was an invisible weight, pressing down on each of us at the table. I shook my head slightly in response to Jaimie, trying to convey my sense of exasperation and helplessness. It wasn't about taking sides in that moment, but rather about navigating the turbulent emotions swirling around us. Momma and Poppa sat at opposite ends of the table, their own emotions simmering beneath the surface, creating an invisible barrier between them.

In that charged moment, it was evident that unresolved tensions and unspoken grievances had erupted to the surface. Each word left unspoken seemed to reverberate loudly in the silence, adding to the growing divide between us all. Momma's retreating figure spoke volumes, her rigid posture and brisk movements reflecting her inner turmoil

The storm raging outside was slowly reduced to a distant memory as we settled in for the night. Or so we thought. Poppa, never one to abandon his routines, pulled out his pack of cigarettes.

"Randolph!" Momma's voice sliced through the cozy calm, her tone sharp as she bounced baby Hayes on her hip. "This is a non-smoking hotel—you can't do that here! The woman at the receptionist's desk was already nice enough to let us stay here for the night "

Poppa rolled his eyes, exhaling with irritation. "So, what am I supposed to do then?"

"It should be obvious," she replied, exasperated. "Go outside! We'll get kicked out if the smoke detector goes off."

Grumbling, Poppa grabbed his jacket and headed into the night. Moments later, Jaimie, my older brother, slipped on his shoes and followed him, the door clicking shut behind him.

Outside, Poppa sank onto the concrete curb, flicking his lighter and taking a long drag, lost in thought. Jaimie settled down beside him, silent at first, then turned, watching Poppa. "Got a lighter?"

Poppa hesitated, the weight of the moment pressing between them. He looked at Jaimie, his expression shadowed with regret as if he could see a younger version of himself reflected in his son's face. After a beat, he handed over the lighter, shoulders sagging with resignation.

They smoked in silence for a while, the wisps of smoke rising into the dark, rainy sky. Finally, Poppa broke the quiet, his voice low and remorseful.

"I'm sorry, Jaimie," he murmured while giving a thousand-yard stare straight ahead of him.

"What are you sorry for?"

"For dragging you into my bad habits. I remember earlier when mom yelled at you for smelling like cigarettes in the car. I stayed silent while you two were yelling at each other but I felt so bad."

There was a pause between them.

"You wouldn't have smelled like cigarettes if I wasn't the one who smoked in front of you and Lilac when you were little." Poppa finished.

Jaimie took a drag, exhaling slowly as he glanced at Poppa. "It's okay. I'm not mad," he said, a small smile tugging at his lips. "I always wanted to be just like you."

Poppa's face softened, but there was a sadness in his eyes. "Yes, but not in this way." He shook his head, flicking ash to the ground. "You should want to be like me for better reasons. I run a business, Jaimie—a business I've worked hard to build, hoping one day you'd want to take it over."

He let out a deep, weary sigh, eyes fixed on the smoky wisps vanishing into the dark. "We are farmers, Jaimie! There was a whole plot of land rich enough to flourish our family for years now, and now it's likely going to be destroyed because of hurricane Irene." Poppa started to look as though he was holding back tears.

For a moment, they both sat in silence, the weight of his words settling between them.

"I'm not mad at you, Jaimie. I'm not." Poppa's voice was soft but heavy with something unspoken. "I'm just angry at myself."

"Dad, I don't think you're giving yourself enough credit," Jaimie replied. "I don't hate you, so that's pretty much 'Dad of the Year' in my book."

Poppa glanced over at Jaimie, who was staring out the window, his face unreadable. Poppa sighed deeply, a sound of weariness that seemed to pull the air from the room. Jaimie let out a long, quiet breath, almost spiritual in its weight.

"Dad?"

"Yes, Jaimie?"

"Are you feeling guilty about smoking in front of me and Lilac because of that argument you had with Mom? The one where she started talking about regretting not going with the Velvet Missiles?"

"Oh. You guys saw that?"

"Yes."

Poppa's hands dropped to his lap, his eyes lost in thought. "Maybe. A little. I don't know."

He rubbed his face with both hands as if trying to wipe away the years of regret. "I just... I feel like such a failure. I remember when your mother first met me. I was so damn insecure. I couldn't understand what a 5'10" model like her saw in a guy like me—a bummy farmer. I didn't feel good enough for her. I still don't."

Poppa," Jaimie said softly, his voice quieter than he intended, "I never knew you thought that. About Mom, I mean."

Poppa blinked as if he hadn't heard his son speak for a moment, then turned his eyes to Jaimie. The vulnerability in his gaze made Jaimie's chest tighten.

"Yeah," Poppa murmured, the weight of his thoughts pulling him deeper into himself. "I don't think I ever told her that. I just... I kept it all inside because I didn't want to seem weak. But every time she'd talk about those days—before we had you guys—she'd get this look in her eyes. Like she was still wondering about what might've been. That's when I started drinking, smoking... whatever it took to drown out the voice in my head telling me I wasn't enough. And I figured, if I didn't talk about it, maybe it'd go away."

Jaimie shifted uncomfortably, not knowing how to fix this. His father had always been the rock, the one who seemed to have all the answers. But this... this side of him was unfamiliar. And it terrified Jaimie to think that Poppa, the man who'd held the family together all these years, felt so small.

"Poppa, you're more than enough," Jaimie said, his voice a little more firm than before. "I mean it. I don't remember a time when you weren't there for me. For Lilac. You've been our rock. It's just... I don't know, Dad. You're human too, you know? And maybe that's okay."

Poppa snorted softly, a bitter sound. "That's the thing, Jaimie. I don't feel human. I feel like I've been pretending for so long that even I don't recognize myself anymore. Do you ever feel like that? Like you're living in some version of yourself that you don't control?"

Jaimie considered the question, his gaze drifting to the window, watching the world blur by as the sun dipped lower in the sky. The tension in the air seemed to stretch for miles, but he couldn't find the words. Not yet.

"Yeah," Jaimie muttered after a long beat. "Yeah, I get that. I think I've felt like that my whole life." He let out a long breath, staring at his reflection in the window as he spoke. "Maybe that's why I hate being told what to do. It feels like someone else is pulling the strings, and I'm just... just the puppet, you know? But then I think about how much worse it would be if you weren't here. Like, what would Mom do? What would Lilac and I do?"

Poppa was silent for a while, then leaned back in his chair, as if the weight of Jaimie's words was finally starting to sink in.

"I guess I never thought about it like that," Poppa said quietly. "I don't know what the hell I'm doing sometimes, Jaimie. I'm just... trying to hold on. Trying to do right by you and your sister. But I'm scared I'm messing it all up. That's why I get so mad. It's not you, it's just... I feel like I've failed you both. I've failed your mom." His voice wavered, and for the first time, Jaimie heard the fragility beneath his father's tough exterior.

Jaimie glanced over at him, swallowing the lump in his throat. "Dad, maybe you can't fix everything. But you're not a failure. You're just a guy who made some mistakes. We all do. We're not perfect, none of us. Hell, I can barely get through a day without screwing something up."

Poppa chuckled softly, but it didn't quite reach his eyes. "You're right about that. But if you guys can't see me as a failure, then maybe... maybe I don't need to see myself that way either."

There was a long pause, and Jaimie felt something shift. A lightness in the room, as if the burden between them had lessened if only a little.

"You're not perfect, Dad," Jaimie said, his voice steady now, "but you've been here. You've always been here. And that's what counts. It's enough."

Poppa looked over at his son, something like relief in his eyes, though still tinged with doubt. "I don't know, Jaimie. I'm just not sure if I can ever make up for all the times I've been lost."

"Maybe you don't have to," Jaimie said. "Maybe we just need you to be here. And maybe that's enough for us too."

For the first time in a long while, Poppa smiled, a slow, hesitant thing, but it was real. And in that moment, Jaimie felt a small flicker of hope, like maybe things didn't have to be perfect to be alright.

They sat there, saying nothing more, just two figures in the dim glow of streetlights, caught in the pull of the impending storm on the outside and the ones within.

Chapter Six: A Dream From Somebody

"The storm continued to rage relentlessly outside the walls of the hotel, its ferocity so intense that it eventually plunged the entire building into darkness. One moment, everything was normal, and then the lights flickered, went out completely, and left us all in shadow. Despite the ominous weather, Poppa and my older brother Jaimie were still outside, chatting away, oblivious to the chaos brewing around us. When they finally stepped inside, they were greeted by the strange sight of the dim, silent hotel lobby. Confusion on their faces, they made their way over to the front desk.

"What's going on?" Poppa asked the receptionist, his voice blending into the low hum of worried chatter in the room.

The woman at the desk looked frazzled but managed a sympathetic smile. "It's Hurricane Irene," she explained, shaking her head. "She's coming in full force—this is just the beginning."

With a glance at each other, Poppa and Jaimie turned back toward the stairs, making their way up to our hotel room. As they entered, Momma looked up, her face half-lit in the soft glow of the flashlight we'd managed to find.

"The TV's out," she said, her tone hovering somewhere between frustration and resignation.

"Yeah," Poppa replied, "the receptionist said it's because of Hurricane Irene."

"So what do we do now?" Momma asked, clearly not a fan of sitting idle.

Poppa shrugged, his usual easygoing attitude evident. "Just sit tight and wait it out, I guess."

And that's what we did. We gathered together in a circle on the hotel room floor, sitting cross-legged, the flickering beam of the flashlight casting long shadows around us. With nothing else to do, we ended up simply staring at each other, a strange silence falling over us as the wind howled outside.

After a moment, I noticed the tattoo on Poppa's left forearm, a design I'd seen countless times but never really thought to ask about. The quiet felt like an invitation, so I finally did.

"Poppa," I said softly, breaking the silence. "What's that tattoo on your arm?"

Poppa looked down at his forearm, running a thumb over the inked skin as if tracing the lines of memory. A small smile tugged at the corner of his mouth before he met my gaze.

"It's a tattoo for a friend I used to have," he replied, his voice carrying a note of warmth and something else—maybe sadness.

"Oh," I murmured, unsure what to say.

After a pause, Poppa continued, his voice growing softer as if speaking more to himself than to us. "His name was Given. We were close. He was the one I planned to start a farm with someday." He chuckled, though the sound was tinged with regret. "We used to talk about it all the time—working the land, building something from the ground up."

The room was quiet as he spoke, everyone listening intently. It was rare for Poppa to open up like this, and I sensed that even Momma was hearing parts of the story she hadn't known before.

"What happened to him?" Jaimie asked, leaning in with curiosity.

Poppa sighed, his gaze distant. "Things changed. Given... he made some choices that took him down a rough path. He ended up in prison." He hesitated, the weight of the words settling over us. "I got this tattoo to remember him. Not because of what he did, but because of who he was to me—my friend, my brother in a way."

The silence returned, but this time it was filled with a new understanding. Poppa's voice softened even more, his hand still absentmindedly tracing the tattoo. "Sometimes, you hold onto people, not for what they did right or wrong, but because they were part of you for a while."

I sat back, processing what he'd said, feeling a mixture of emotions.

"What happened to Given that caused him to end up in prison?" Jaimie asked.

Poppa took a moment to think.

"It wasn't his fault that caused him to be in prison," Poppa explained. "It was more so the state. There was a recent case of someone stealing, and they just needed to pin someone to the crime. So that was where Given became the victim of the system. He didn't have a family rich enough to fight for him, so he got sent into a penitentiary."

Just then, Jaimie spoke up, "Did you ever think about visiting him?"

Poppa shook his head, his eyes still on the tattoo. "I thought about it, sure. But some things... they're just too hard to face."

After sitting together in that circle for a while, we all grew tired and drifted off to the hotel beds, each of us quietly processing the evening's stories. That night, when I lay down, I had a dream—a strange, vivid one. I rarely ever dream, and if I do, I hardly remember them. But this one felt different. It lingered.

In my dream, I found myself running through a vast, empty field. The ground was pure white, stretching endlessly in all directions, like a blank canvas.

The sky was the perfect shade of blue, a serene backdrop to the seemingly endless terrain where I found myself running. Despite its vastness, a clear boundary was present, marked by a sturdy wall complete with guardhouse towers positioned strategically at each corner. The sight was peculiar; an air of protection enveloped the area, yet I stood alone in its expanse. It was just me, surrounded by the silent sentinels. Suddenly, a series of flickering candles materialized, forming a guiding path that beckoned for me to follow. The warm glow they emitted seemed to promise direction, drawing me further into this mysterious space.

The air was silent and heavy, and each step I took seemed to echo in the stillness. Then, out of nowhere, I saw him.

A tall man with dark skin stood and a scar on his forehead in the distance, perfectly still, almost as if he'd been waiting for me. I slowed my steps and approached him cautiously. When I got close enough to see his face, he looked down at me, a quiet intensity in his eyes.

"Oh," I said, feeling the weight of his words settles between us.

He tilted his head, a hint of curiosity in his eyes. "And what's your name?"

"My name is Lilac. My mother loves flowers. She says I reminded her of one."

"Lilac," he repeated with a faint smile. "That's beautiful."

"Thank you," I replied, smiling back. A silence fell, delicate and lingering, and I sensed that he was about to slip away. Suddenly, a surge of panic rose in me.

"Wait!" I called out, reaching out instinctively. "Why did you come into my dream just now?"

He paused as if weighing how much to tell me. "It's because of this hotel you're staying in."

"What about it?" I pressed.

"It's cursed," he said, his words heavy.

A chill ran through me. "Why do you say that?"

"This place," he began, his voice laced with sorrow, "was built on the backs of slaves. They poured their labor into every stone, every wall, but they were never given credit, never acknowledged for what they built. Their spirits linger, restless."

Restless?" I echoed, feeling a shiver despite the warmth of the room. "Do they... haunt this place?"

"In a way," Given replied, his gaze distant, as if he could see things I couldn't. "Their anger and sorrow linger. It's woven into the walls, into the very foundation. Those who stay here sometimes sense it, even if they don't understand what they're feeling."

"Have you... seen them?" I asked, my voice barely above a whisper.

Given nodded slowly. "I've felt them. Heard them, too. Sometimes, late at night, if you listen closely, you might hear faint whispers or feel a cold breeze even when the windows are shut."

A heavy silence settled between us as I took in his words. "But why me?" I finally asked. "Why did you come to me?"

"You're more open than most," Given said, his gaze softening. "You're connected to something beyond yourself—something that allows you to sense things others might overlook."

I swallowed, feeling both unsettled and oddly comforted by his presence. "What... what do they want?"

"They want peace," he said simply. "Recognition. And justice for what was taken from them. Some of them may never find rest until the truth of their suffering is acknowledged."

A faint sense of resolve stirred within me. "Is there anything I can do to help them?"

Given looked at me thoughtfully, as if surprised by my willingness. "There might be. Sometimes, bringing light to hidden truths is all it takes. If people knew, really knew, about what happened here... maybe it would bring some peace."

I nodded slowly, feeling a new weight settle on my shoulders. "Then I'll do it," I whispered. "I'll find a way to let people know. To tell their story."

A faint smile crossed his lips, and there was something almost relieved in his eyes. "Thank you, Lilac."

Just then, a gust of cold air swept through the room, and I felt the faintest hint of a presence behind me, something unseen but deeply felt. I turned back to Given, but he had already begun to fade, his figure becoming less defined, his edges blurring like smoke.

"Wait!" I called, panic rising in me. "Will I see you again?"

"Maybe," he replied, his voice echoing faintly, as though from a great distance. "If you need me... I'll find you."

A strange warmth filled me, a feeling I couldn't quite place—like I'd known him all along, even though we'd never met. I wanted to ask him more, to understand why he was here, but before I could say another word, the field began to fade, the white stretching out into shadows. I reached for him, but he was already slipping away, his figure dissolving into the mist.

And then I woke up, the remnants of the dream fading as I opened my eyes. But his name, *Given*, stayed with me, lingering in my mind like a whispered secret.

I was the only one awake in the hotel room. I glanced over at Poppa, asleep beside Momma, and my older brother Jaimie, who lay curled up next to me. Baby Hayes was sleeping soundly on the floor in his little rocker, his breathing soft and steady. Careful not to wake anyone else, I slipped out of bed and tiptoed over to Poppa's side. Gently, I reached out and shook his shoulder.

"Poppa," I whispered. "Wake up, please."

He stirred, slowly opening his eyes. "Lilac?" he asked, his voice laced with sleep and concern. "What's the matter?"

"It's Given," I murmured. "I saw him in my dreams."

"Given?" He blinked, rubbing his eyes. "How did you know it was him?"

"He told me his name," I explained. "And he had a mark on his forehead."

Poppa looked at me, his eyes narrowing slightly. "How did you know Given had a mark on his forehead?"

I shrugged, a little smile tugging at my lips. "Maybe... that's how you'd know it was him."

He paused, thinking, then nodded slowly. "Alright, Lilac. What did he say to you?"

"He told me this hotel is haunted," I whispered urgently. "He thinks we should leave."

Poppa sat up, his face now serious. Without a word, he shook Momma gently awake, then turned to rouse Jaimie. One by one, we all quietly gathered our things and left the room. Soon, we were in the car, driving down the empty road, the hotel fading into the darkness behind us.

Chapter Seven: Uncle Randy's

After what felt like an eternity we finally arrived at Uncle Randy's house, greeted by the warm glow of porch lights casting a welcoming light on our weary faces. The sense of relief and anticipation mingled in the air, a culmination of the road traveled and the destination ahead, promising moments of shared joy and cherished memories in the company of loved ones. The echoes of our journey reverberated in my mind, each mile serving as a testament to the resilience and camaraderie that defined our shared adventure, a journey that transcended mere distance to become a tapestry of experiences woven with threads of connection, discovery, and the enduring spirit of exploration.

He and our cousins welcomed us warmly at the door, their faces lighting up with joy at our arrival. They eagerly assisted us in unloading our suitcases and bags from the car.

The genuine smiles and warm expressions on their faces nearly made the dramatic journey worthwhile. Auntie Raya, the wife of Uncle Randy, set up a cozy crib for baby boy Hayes in his very own room. Meanwhile, Jaimie and I found ourselves sharing bunk beds with our cousins. To my surprise, my cousin Britney offered to carry my suitcase. She usually gave off an air of being too sophisticated for such tasks, so her willingness to help caught me off guard.

I admired her greatly; she embodied everything I aspired to be. Britney was the glamorous and affluent cousin I often envied. She always had a delightful fragrance, consistently made the honor roll with straight A's, and excelled in basketball and baseball. I couldn't blame her for her aloofness or for only helping those who explicitly asked for it. She had every right to carry herself with a bit of pride. Still, when she offered to carry my luggage, it revealed that she actually might have admired me in a way too.

Jaime and I walk inside Uncle Randy's house, marveling at its grandeur and vastness. The spacious rooms and high ceilings were a stark contrast to the coziness of our humble abode. We couldn't help but notice the intricate details in the architecture and the elegant decor that adorned every corner. As we explored further, we couldn't help but feel a sense of awe at the sheer size and opulence of Uncle Randy's house. It was like stepping into a different world, one filled with luxury and sophistication that we were not accustomed to in our own smaller, more modest dwelling. The walls seemed to echo our footsteps, emphasizing just how much larger and more expansive this house was compared to our own. Looking around, we couldn't help but feel a mixture of admiration and a twinge of envy at Uncle Randy's impressive home. However, despite the grandeur and magnificence of his house, we also couldn't help but appreciate the warmth and comfort that our own smaller home provided, knowing that it was filled with love and cherished memories that no grandeur could ever replace.

Britney kindly guided me to our designated room within the house where we would be staying for the weekend. To my surprise, the room held a cozy bunk bed that we would be sharing. Meanwhile, Britney's younger brother, Aiden, accompanied Jaimie to the room assigned to them as both boys would be sharing the space. Given that Jaimie and Aiden were boys and thus needed to share a room, it made perfect sense for Britney and me to also be roommates during our stay.

Additionally, it was planned that our parents, Momma and Poppa, would be occupying the basement area for the duration of our visit. While Britney graciously assisted me in unpacking my luggage, we engaged in a delightful conversation that helped us get to know each other better and fostered a sense of camaraderie between us.

As I carefully unpacked my belongings, my attention was gradually drawn towards Britney, who was meticulously folding her clothes with remarkable precision. The sight of her perfectly aligned corners and seamless creases as she folded each garment flawlessly sparked a tinge of annoyance within me. I couldn't help but marvel at her methodical approach to organizing her wardrobe, each item neatly arranged with an almost artistic flair. The contrast between her meticulous folding technique and my more haphazard method made me reassess my approach to tidying up. I let out a sigh in frustration.

"What's the matter, Lilac?" Cousin Britney asked.

"Oh, it's nothing," I responded. "It's just that you know, you fold the clothes so perfectly. I don't even know why I bother trying. You're so good at everything."

Britney let out a belly laugh in response.

"Well, I don't know about everything, Lilac. I just..I don't know, I've always had to make sure I did everything right."

"Well from the way I see things, you don't have to try. You're already like...perfect." I glance at Britney a little bit annoyed. "You're pretty, you're good at sports, you always smell like cinnamon. I bet Uncle Randy and Auntie Raya are proud of you."

I noticed Britney pause for a moment, her smile faltering.

"What? You don't think that that's true?" I asked her.

"I mean maybe. But that's kind of...part of the problem. It's like they always expect me to be good at everything, all the time. I can't take an off day or a break without feeling as though I'm letting them down."

I was pleasantly surprised when Britney said that to me.

"Really? I thought you just liked being perfect."

Britney let out another sigh as she folded another one of my shirts carefully.

"Sometimes I wish I didn't have to be. Every grade, every game, even how I look. It's like everyone is just waiting for the moment that I slip up. And when I do slip up, they look at me like I committed a crime. It's all so exhausting."

My face softened when Britney told me that. I could feel the jealousy in my body start to fade a little bit.

"That sounds...a lot harder than I thought. I guess I didn't think about the expectations that would come with being known for being good at something."

"Yeah. I mean don't get me wrong. I'm grateful for a lot of things. But sometimes I just want to be, you know, normal. Like, make a mistake without feeling it would be the end of the world."

"I guess it's not all that fun being perfect," I say while slowly nodding my head.

Britney smiled at me. "No, not really. Sometimes I wish I could just...relax a little. Not worry about what anyone else thinks. Like right now, just hanging out with you - this is nice. No pressure. Just...us."

I paused for a moment to think. "I never really thought about it like that. I always just...I don't know...figured that it was easy for you."

"I get it. I guess I just don't talk about it much. Everyone always sees what's on the outside. Y'know? It's easier to let people think you got it all together."

I hesitated to say what I wanted to say next. "Well, maybe you don't have to pretend all the time."

"That's nice, but with you?"

"With me. I'm not going to judge you if you're not perfect."

Britney smiled a little bit. I could tell she was starting to feel a bit relieved. "Thanks, Lilac. It's nice to hear you say that. I'm so used to trying to meet everyone's expectations, sometimes I forget I don't have to be perfect with the people who care about me."

I smiled back at Britney. "Yeah. Besides, it makes me feel better to know you're a human and you're not some kind of a superhero."

Britney started laughing. "Not. I mess up more than you'd think. I just...hide it well."

"Well next time you need to be imperfect, you can do it around me." I let out a little smirk. "I'll just remind you of that one time you gave that one boy that you liked a peanut chocolate bar, while he was allergic to peanut butter."

Britney let out a groan, but it was a playful expression. "Oh wow, you're never going to let that go now, are you?"

"Never," I responded. We both started laughing even more after that. I could feel the tension between us start to ease.

"Thanks, Lilac. Really. It's nice to just...be myself for once and not have to filter myself in anyways." Britney smiled warmly at me.

"Anytime." I pause, thinking for a moment. "You know, maybe we both need a little time to decompose and let up on ourselves a little bit. I'm so busy worrying about not being like you, I forget that maybe...maybe I'm fine as I am too."

"You are, Lilac," Britney said with a nod. "And if I can be honest, sometimes I wish I could be more like you too."

I was so shocked when Britney said that to me. "Like me? What for?"

"You're...authentic. You don't try to be something you're not. That's something I wish I could do more of."

I smiled at Britney, feeling touched by her words. "Well, I guess we both have a little bit of something that the other one wants."

Britney nodded. "Yeah. Maybe that's what makes us...us."

We shared a smile with each other. That was the moment when we realized we both did not have to be so hard on each other - or even each other. Me and Britney shared a deep hug. Our energies were telepathically being exchanged between us. Then suddenly, that's when Aiden and Jaimie burst into the room and interrupted the moment that we were having.

"Ugh, what do you want, Aiden?" Britney asked with obvious annoyance in her voice.

"Mom said that dinner downstairs is ready," Aiden said matter of fact.

Britney let out a sigh and rolled her eyes as she released me from the hug. "Great. You couldn't have knocked or something?"

Aiden just shrugged, clearly unfazed. "I did. You just didn't hear me because you were busy having some... 'telepathic energy exchange,'" he teased, wiggling his fingers in the air for effect.

Britney's cheeks flushed. "Very funny, Aiden. Not everything's a joke, you know."

Aiden smirked. "Lighten up, Brit. You're too serious all the time." Then he glanced at me, raising an eyebrow. "So, what's the deep, telepathic conversation about anyway? You two are plotting world domination or something?"

I shot him a look, half-amused, half-irritated. "Something like that," I said, playing along. "But you wouldn't understand, Aiden. It's... cousin stuff."

He put his hands up in mock surrender. "Alright, alright. I get it. Secret cousin stuff." Then he looked over his shoulder. "But if you don't hurry, Jamie's gonna finish off all the mashed potatoes."

Britney sighed, her shoulders finally relaxing. "Alright, fine. We're coming."

Aiden turned to leave, but he paused at the door, looking back at Britney with an unusually serious expression. "Hey... just so you know, you don't have to be perfect all the time. Nobody expects you to be, Brit."

Britney looked taken aback, her annoyance replaced by surprise. "Thanks... Aiden."

He gave a small, sincere nod, then his usual grin returned. "See you downstairs," he said, and with that, he was gone.

As soon as he left, Britney turned to me, a soft smile on her face. "Who would've thought? My little brother has a heart."

I chuckled. "He's full of surprises. Just like someone else I know."

Britney smirked, nudging me with her elbow. "Yeah, yeah. Let's go before Jamie does eat all the mashed potatoes."

And together, we headed downstairs, feeling lighter than we had in a long time.

Auntie Raya, with her apron tied securely around her waist, was stationed downstairs in the cozy kitchen, her experienced hands carefully stirring the simmering pot of aromatic stew. As the mouthwatering scents wafted through the air, Momma bustled around the room, lending a helping hand to the bustling preparations. Peeking around the corner, I couldn't help but feel a hint of exasperation flicker within me. Aiden's earlier insistence that dinner was almost ready had been nothing but a mischievous fib, causing a surge of annoyance to bubble up as I realized the truth - the delectable meal we had been eagerly anticipating was not yet prepared.

The sight of Auntie Raya diligently cooking away in the kitchen meant one thing - a delay in our delightful family dinner time. With a resigned sigh, I understood that we would have to pitch in to set the table, my initial reluctance morphing into a begrudging acceptance of the extra effort required. Despite my wavering mood, the thought of gathering around the table with loved ones soon tempered my annoyance, reminding me of the warmth and joy shared during these family feasts.

Embracing the familiar routine of preparing for the meal ahead, I begrudgingly made my way to the dining area, mentally bracing myself for the task at hand. The clinking of cutlery and rustling of napkins soon filled the air as I set about arranging the table. ,

It seemed as though staying at Uncle Randy's house would not be as bad as I was anticipating.

Chapter Eight: The Wind

I couldn't stop thinking about the dream where Given visited me and told me that the hotel my family was staying in was haunted by the spirits of enslaved people who had built it from the ground up. I sat at a desk, working on a personal computer — a large, boxy model, the DataPoint 2022. It took up a significant portion of the desk, with its bulky design and flickering screen. Inspired by Given's words, I decided to write an article for the local newspaper about the history of Sunset Lodge Inn.

I dove into extensive research on the hotel, and what I uncovered confirmed what Given had said. The hotel's history was more sinister than I'd ever imagined. I was determined to use my article to raise awareness about this forgotten chapter of history, ensuring that those who had built the hotel were finally given the recognition they deserved.

I must have been typing away for hours because, eventually, my stomach rumbled, pulling me away from my thoughts. Realizing I couldn't work on an empty stomach, I stood up and headed downstairs to grab a meal, my mind still swirling with everything I had uncovered.

Auntie Raya was busy preparing fish for dinner, while Uncle Randy glanced down at baby Hayes.

""Have you all decided on a name for him yet?" he inquired, eyes sparkling with anticipation. Momma exchanged a loving glance with Hayes, a smile tugging at her lips before she turned her attention back to Randy. "No, we haven't," she replied softly, her voice filled with a mix of uncertainty and longing. "So, what's the hold-up?" Randy persisted, his curiosity piqued by the mystery surrounding the yet-unnamed baby. Momma's gaze drifted to the swaying branches outside the window, a wistful expression crossing her face. "We just can't seem to find the right name," she admitted, a hint of frustration lacing her words. Poppa joined the conversation, his voice gentle but firm as he added, "We want it to be something special, something he can carry with pride his whole life through."

Feeling a sudden surge of determination, I scooped baby Hayes into my arms, feeling his soft breath against my chest as we stepped outside into the embrace of the lively wind. The trees sang a melodious tune, their branches swaying in a mesmerizing dance that echoed the joy bubbling within my heart. Hayes giggled in response, his laughter a melody that blended seamlessly with the wind's soothing whispers. It was in that enchanting moment that inspiration struck like a bolt of lightning, illuminating the path to the perfect name. A name as unique and beautiful as the wind itself. "Zephyr," I declared, my voice resonating with certainty as I met his curious gaze. It was a name that would carry him through every adventure yet to come.

"From now on, your name is Zephyr."

About the Author

Libelle Marcellus is a versatile author with a passion for storytelling across every genre. From a young age, Libelle Marcellus has been creating books and stories, starting at just five years old. This early spark for writing has grown into a lifelong dedication to the craft. Each book is a product of her imagination and hard work—no ghostwriters, just genuine passion and original ideas. Whether crafting heartfelt dramas, thrilling mysteries, or fantastical adventures, she thrives on pushing creative boundaries and bringing fresh perspectives to readers of all kinds.

www.ingramcontent.com/pod-product-compliance
Lightning Source LLC
Chambersburg PA
CBHW020646160726
47991CB00003B/1054